KLEPT🐾DOGS

WHO LET THE PUPS OUT

By Daphne Pendergrass

KleptoDogs™ & HyperBeard®.
All rights reserved. Published by Scholastic Inc., *Publishers since 1920*.
SCHOLASTIC and associated logos are trademarks and/or registered trademarks of Scholastic Inc.

The publisher does not have any control over and does not assume any responsibility for author or third-party websites or their content.

This book is a work of fiction. Names, characters, places, and incidents are either the product of the author's imagination or are used fictitiously, and any resemblance to actual persons, living or dead, business establishments, events, or locales is entirely coincidental.

ISBN 978-1-338-55604-9

10 9 8 7 6 5 4 3 2   19 20 21 22 23

Printed in the U.S.A.   40
First printing 2019

Book design by Jessica Meltzer
Illustrated by Andrea Mendoza Melgarejo

TABLE OF CONTENTS

THE LEGEND OF GEMDOG

Welcome, fren! If you're here, that means you've met the Very Good Bois, otherwise known as the KleptoDogs! These mischievous little puppers are sure to steal your heart faster than they can steal your sandwich. (And trust us, they can steal your sandwich pretty fast.)

By now we're sure you have more questions than you can shake a stick at. Lucky for you, this guide is here to help you through your journey with the KleptoDogs. Before we get too far, let's rewind and go back to where it all began, with this little pup known as GemDog . . .

IN THE BEGINNING, there were the KleptoCats. Wise and all-seeing, they traveled the multiverse, using their interdimensional portals to steal anything they wanted—objects, people, snakes—from not just their own time and space, but from the future, past, and different dimensions as well. They fought in great wars and laid siege to their enemies, the Hamsters.

BUT ONE DAY, Guapo, the heroic leader of the KleptoCats, found something quite unexpected in a very ordinary home: a dog. (But, like, a really cute dog.) Guapo framed this dog for stealing its owner's sandwich. When the poor boi was kicked outside, Guapo used the stolen sandwich to lure the pup into a portal.

9

GUAPO TOOK GEMDOG on as a personal apprentice. The pupper didn't have a natural desire to steal (except when it came to food), but it did love to fetch and dig. When the pup's natural abilities were honed, the KleptoCats taught GemDog how to travel by magical portal and set it (mostly) free. GemDog in turn spread the knowledge of the portals to its people, the Very Good Bois.

ON THE OTHER side of the portal, this best boi was reborn. It became known as Gem-Dog, the beloved pet of Guapo and the KleptoCats. The cats were in awe of this strange creature. Unlike them, it was not stealthy or clever. It could not sneak about unnoticed, stealing for them. Still, Guapo saw a great future for GemDog.

MANY KLEPTOCATS DIDN'T think it was possible for GemDog to master their art of stealing really GOOD stuff. But GemDog proved them wrong, becoming the general for a new adorable army. For what the Very Good Bois lacked in stealth (and intelligence), they made up for in OVERWHELMING cuteness. Humans who find the KleptoDogs up to no good are charmed by every . . .

FLOOFER,

THE VERY GOOD BOIS

Similar to KleptoCats, KleptoDogs come in many different colors. But did you know they come in different shapes and sizes too? No two puppers are the same! The Very Good Bois are always welcoming new KleptoDogs to their posse, but we've rounded up the very best in this section!

GEMDOG

- It learned from the best, and now it's ready to lead.

- First non-cat being to be accepted among the KleptoCats.

- Bonded with Guapo over their mutual love of sandwiches.

- Has never once chased its tail.

- A tree it peed on became a national landmark.

- Will defend its house from any foe. Except the vacuum.

- Made frenz with the help of its excellent bork.

THE BACKYARD DOGS

FLOP

- It has two left feet.
- Loves chewing on your dancing shoes.

CORGS

- It literally means dwarf dog.
- Its ears are radar dishes.

DOTS

- Prefers ice cream in nontraditional ways.
- Super good at tic-tac-toe.

KYUNAE
- It's a really big fan of speedy hedgehogs.
- Its cousin was a fox.

FERNO
- Likes to sunbathe for hours on end.
- Warmest pup in the tristate area.

SUBY
- Was lost in the city so it called a taxi.
- Its hobbies include licking feet.

MIKI
- Enjoys knitting in the middle of the night.
- Borks for dramatic effect.

19

THE KITCHEN DOGS

TOXIC
- Likes to roll around in things it probably shouldn't.
- Its DNA is being studied for science.

SODA
- Enjoys an unhealthy dose of sugar on a regular basis.
- Chases after bugs for exercise.

LADY
- Doesn't need a tramp to know its own worth.
- Likes to investigate strange smells.

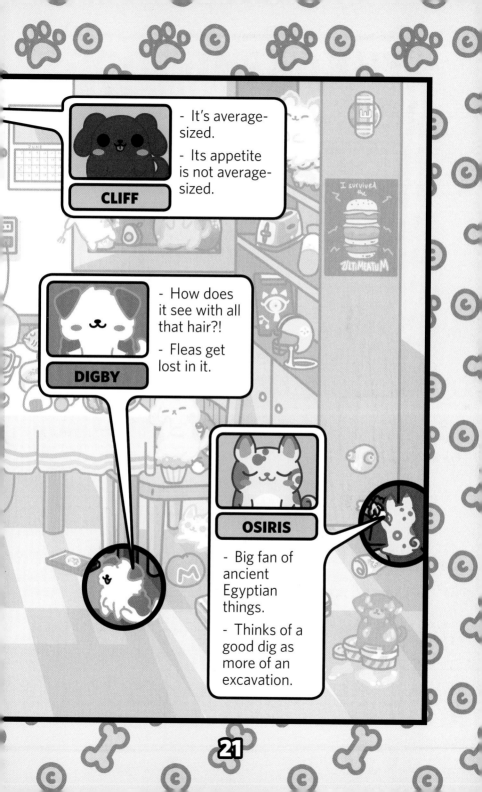

CLIFF

- It's average-sized.
- Its appetite is not average-sized.

DIGBY

- How does it see with all that hair?!
- Fleas get lost in it.

OSIRIS

- Big fan of ancient Egyptian things.
- Thinks of a good dig as more of an excavation.

THE GARAGE DOGS

YANKO

- Likes chocolate milkshakes.
- Could pull a sled . . . if it wanted to.

SAMURAI

- It trusts only a few.
- Snores so loud it wakes itself up.

CHIEF

- It's nothing without Cortana.
- Enjoys ketchup way more than mustard. Don't get us started on relish.

DAN
- Silly and cute.
- Has a collection of googly eyes.

XENON
- Has noble farts.
- Makes frenz easily.

CHEWIE
- Is in love with its ball.
- Throws its ball under the furniture for attention.

MS. MOLLY
- It's a cute corgi.
- Once got into glitter and had sparkly poops for a week.

DIAGRAM OF A KLEPTODOG

PUPPY DOG EYES

If you see a KleptoDog shamefully avoiding eye contact . . . it's usually the first sign that your pup got into something. You'll see the telltale sad, glassy KleptoDog's eyes that read "Not me . . ."

SNOOT

Snoots come in all shapes and sizes. Some KleptoDogs' snoots are long and pointy while others are short and flat. Either way, all pups' snoots should be touched with one finger, otherwise known as a "boop," as in "boop the snoot."

PANTALOONS

Many KleptoDogs have a thick layer of fur on the backs of their legs known as pantaloons. These pantaloons keep pups warm and speedy.

FUN-O-METER

More wags means more fun.

TOE BEANS

Flip a pup's paw and you'll find the toe beans! Though they are called "beans," they are not for eating. They are for helping a pupper get where it needs to go.

BINGO

That's the spot, right there.

KLEPTODOG BREEDS

Unlike KleptoCats, KleptoDogs come in different categories called breeds. From floofers to shoobs to corgos to wrinklers, here we cover the breeds you need to know about!

PUPPERS

Puppers are your standard KleptoDog. They're medium-sized and produce a medium bork. Their fur is short, and their ears are nice and floppy. Young puppers love mischief. Beware their hypnotic eyes, which can lead you to do all sorts of things, like feed them dinner scraps or buy them rather expensive toys.

LONG BOIS

Long Bois are long and (usually) skinny dogs. They tend to burrow and can morph into blanket creatures. Never disturb a burrowing long boi, as they have a tendency to become quite snarly when comfortable. Not to be confused with chunky corgos.

FLOOFERS

Floofers are exactly what they sound like . . . floofy. Their voluminous, tufted fur is soft as a cloud and is equally nice to touch. With these pups you'll likely want to keep a shedding brush handy, but NOT a vacuum. Floofers and vacuums are sworn enemies. There is that rare floofer who will allow its owner to vacuum it directly, but this is not recommended.

KLEPTODOG BREEDS

YAPPERS

Yappers are the littlest pups who tend to make a yip or yap sound. Unlike many other KleptoDog breeds, yappers' eyes are actually bigger than their stomachs. Yappers tend to gravitate to higher spaces—like the back of a couch, or Mt. Everest—since they want to be at or above your eye level. Don't let them jump from high places, though; they overestimate their abilities.

CORGOS

These long, chunky dogs have a foxy face and short legs. Corgos will often lay in the "full sploot" position, with their stubby little legs splayed behind them. Corgos have a special "derp" ability, which is usually activated in moments of intense games of fetch. But beware— extreme derping can lead to malfunction. If this happens, reset your corgo with belly rubs.

SHOOBS

Similar to the corgo, the shoob is another foxy dog who has normal-sized legs and poofier, floofier fur. A loveable, if quite mysterious, breed, shoobs have been known to express extreme disapproval. If you or someone you know has been a victim of a disappointed shoob, don't wait. Reach out to friends, family, and other KleptoDogs for support.

KLEPTODOG BREEDS

PUGGOS

These pudgy little puppers are easy to please and care for. A group of happy puggos is called a "puggorade," not to be confused with a "puggoraid," which is what happens when all your stuff is stolen by a group of puggos. They love to laze about the house, especially on Wednesdays. Hump-day . . . am I right?!

WOOFERS

Woofers are big bois (not to be confused with boofers, or sub-woofers, who are really big bois). They have a loud, deep bork and are very, very strong. But woofers are gentle giants who sometimes don't know their own strength. Beware their big prances, which can trample normal humans.

BOOFERS (SUB-WOOFERS)

Boofers, sometimes known as sub-woofers, are Really Big KleptoDogs. Despite their large size, do not ride about on their backs—they still have pride. Boofers can pull you around, though. As the saying goes, a boofer walks you, not the other way around.

WRINKLERS

These pups are born with fur that folds up into layers and layers of wrinkles. Don't worry, your pup is not aging rapidly—this is just how they are. When wrinklers are young, they can be quite self-conscious of their folds. Reassure them of their cuteness with head pats and extra treats to help them grow into their wrinkles.

KLEPTODOG OWNER'S MANUAL

As we're sure you know by now, the KleptoDogs are quite different from the KleptoCats. While the cats can handle themselves for the most part, these puppers need lots of love and attention to not totally destroy your stuff, get stuck in strange places, or otherwise cause kanine chaos. Get to know your pups' special needs in this section!

BORKING GUIDE

KleptoDogs have a wide range of borks, each of which means something slightly different.

Scerred Bork

Translation: Hello. I am not sure how I got up here, but I want down please yes please.

Whiny Bork/Scratch

Translation: Please. I am pathetic. I am able to open interdimensional portals, but this is a *door*. You cannot expect me to get past this.

BORKING GUIDE

Yipe Bork

Translation: I thought I made a new fren, but it's too prickly.

Muffled Bork

Translation: I dug too deep and fell in. It's dark. Help?

Defensive Bork

Translation: We are being INVADED. MAN YOUR BATTLE STATIONS. PREPARE TO FIGHT.

Silence

Translation: It's . . . too quiet. What are they up to now?

BUILDING A NUTRITIOUS DIET FOR YOUR KLEPTODOGS

Start with the basics.

Keep them away from junk food.

Consider adding something new and healthy to their diet.

But then again, a little sandwich never hurt anyone.

SIX VERY GOOD BOIS WHO HAVE NO IDEA WHAT THEY'RE DOING

These puppers are all trying very hard not to fall.

This floof is about to bite off more than it can chew.

This pup wanted some light reading and ended up with a bird instead.

This pup just wants to make a new fren.

KLEPTODOG BEDTIME STORIES

Once upon a time, there were two frenz but only one slice of pizza.

The end.

There once was a pupper whose human refused to give it table scraps.

The pup was so hungry that it became a skeleton pup. The end. What a bad human.

KLEPTODOG BEDTIME STORIES

There once was a pup who could stand on its head.

It was so talented that it was crowned king for life. The end.

Once upon a time, there lived a
yapper and a vacuum . . .

Too scary, huh? Never mind. The end.

KLEPTODOGS' MOOD CHART

Scrunch: Feed me now or I will die.

Stretch: Ready for playtime.

Sploot: Playtime over.
Commence laze mode.

Reach: You has food up there?!

THREE REASONS KLEPTODOGS SHOULD NEVER BE ALLOWED TO DRIVE

They'd hold up traffic.

All heck would break loose as soon as they saw a squirrel.

Too many car chases.

WHY KLEPTODOGS' LIVES ARE BETTER WITH MAGIC PORTALS

Infinite tail-chasing.

Meeting interesting new people . . .
or creatures? Not sure what that is.

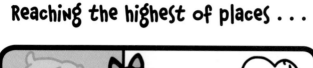

Reaching the highest of places . . .

. . . including the highest of places with
the yummiest of foods.

EXERCISING YOUR KLEPTODOGS

Invest in quality
workout equipment.

Try a new sport.

Give them challenging puzzles to keep them mentally stimulated.

When all else fails, just let them chase each other around the house.

KLEPTODOGS' STRANGE BEHAVIORS REVEALED!

WINKING

It doesn't actually mean anything.
You don't have to wink back.

CIRCLING

This is a precise mathematical calculation to achieve the optimal ratio of cuteness to available space.

WHINING

There are so many good smells out there! But it's nice and safe in here! Decisions!

BORKING (at nothing)

Oh no. There is *something*. You just can't smell it. Or hear it. Or see it.

GROOMING YOUR PUPS

When it's looking like your pup might have gotten into something it shouldn't have, it's time for a bath.

Do *not* let them groom themselves. They may try to kiss you afterward.

Gather your soap and loofah, and wrangle your pup. Keep in mind that it may be well camouflaged.

Scrub all the grime away until your pup is sparkly clean!

PHRASES YOUR DOG WILL MISINTERPRET

WHAT YOU SAY: "Time to go to the vet!"
WHAT THEY THINK: *Why do you hate me?! What did I do?*

WHAT YOU SAY: "Sit, pup!"
WHAT THEY THINK: *Why yes, in fact I can dance! Watch me go . . .*

WHAT YOU SAY: "IS there Someone at the door?"

WHAT THEY THINK: WE ARE UNDER SIEGE. MAN YOUR BATTLE STATIONS!

WHAT YOU SAY: "uh uh uh. This is not for puppies."

WHAT THEY THINK: This is for me. Why thank you! You shouldn't have.

PHRASES YOUR DOG WILL INTERPRET MORE CORRECTLY

WHAT YOU SAY: "Time to vacuum!"
WHAT THEY THINK: *RUN AwAyyyyyyy!!!!!*

WHAT YOU SAY: "what a beautiful day to go outside on a . . ."
WHAT THEY THINK: *WALK! way ahead of you. I'll grab the leash.*

WHAT YOU SAY: "Ugh, leftovers again . . ."
WHAT THEY THINK: *DINNERTIME!*

WHAT YOU SAY: "Who's a Good Boi!"
WHAT THEY THINK: *TREAT TIME!!!!*

STEP-BY-STEP GUIDE TO USING MAGIC PORTALS

Step 1: Open magic portal into moving car.

Step 2: Enjoy.

Step 1: Open magic portal into butcher shop.

Step 2: Enjoy.

FETCH!

We know that caring for the KleptoDogs is hard work, but all that work is sure to pay off as soon as they start bringing things back for you. Check out all the amazing things your puppers will bring in this section.

KLEPTODOGS GO ANTIQUING!

Unidentifiable Skull:
Really old. Smells funny.

Worth: Priceless

Cool Car: Pup-mobile.
If it fits, we sits.

Worth: $100,000

A Really, Really Good Hiding Place:
Perfect for Scaring cats.

Worth: $3,842.67 x 10^{10}

Square watermelon:
May have unique flavor.
But also has Suspicious ears.

Worth: ???

KLEPTODOGS RATE STUFF

Fountain:
Such majestic. Grand. Much inspire.
To pee.

11/10

Comfy Cozy Couch Chair:
Much Snooze. ZzZzZzZzZ . . .

14/10

Giant Dog Bowl:
Oh WOW! Such foods . . . can't reach.
Much Sad.

6/10

CLIFF's

KLEPTODOGS RATE STUFF

Pool Noodle:
Purple Stick! Much fetch. Too big.
Small mouth. Sad.

8/10

Lizard Fren:
New Fren! Much Scales. Looks Nice.

13/10

Spilled Popcorn:
Butter + Salt + Floor = Perfection.

16/10

Wishing Well:
Many pups. Such wish. Fall in. So sad.

2/10

LIFE WITH KLEPTODOGS: EXPECTATION VS. REALITY

EXPECTATION: Fluffy, floofy pups everywhere!

REALITY: Fluffy, floofy, hairy, sticky, smelly, disgusting fur . . . everywhere :(

EXPECTATION: Pups dozing peacefully by your bedside.

REALITY: Total CHAOS! KleptoDogs sleep in shifts.

LIFE WITH KLEPTODOGS: EXPECTATION VS. REALITY

EXPECTATION: Feeding time with loads of pups eating neatly side by side.

REALITY: Why is there so much ice cream on the floor?!

EXPECTATION: Peaceful mornings with a cuddly pup by your side.

REALITY: Where's Chewie? Is he . . . NO, did he . . . did he REALLY just pee on his collar . . . AGAIN?!

PLANNING A PARTY FOR YOUR KLEPTODOGS

Are your pups feeling restless lately? Throw them a party to help them let off some steam! Just follow these simple steps:

1. Buy Some party favors. The bigger the better.

2. Get a pup or two to man the grill.

3. Turn on some rockin' tunes.

4. Invest in boxes for maximum pup entertainment!

FRAGILE

COOKING WITH KLEPTODOGS

Do your research. *Become* the food.

Gather all the ingredients.

Don't be afraid to mix it up.

Enjoy the fruits of your labor.

NO: A HOLIDAY PLAY IN FOUR ACTS

No.

No.

No!

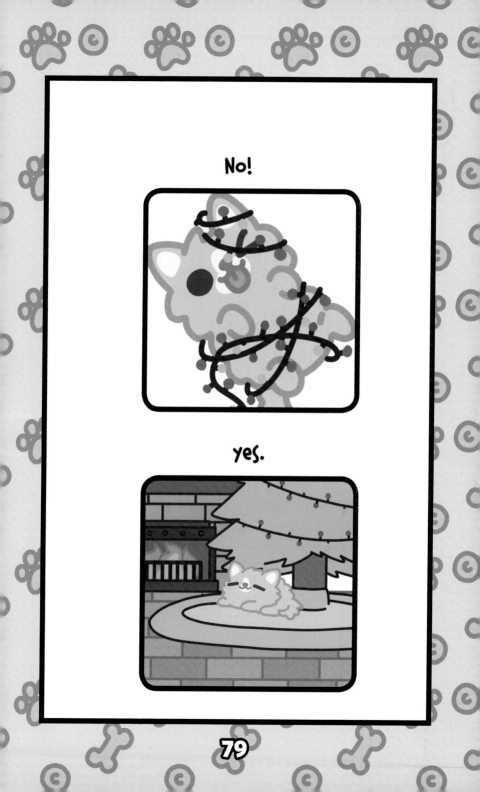

yes.

4: Depression

5: Acceptance

KLEPTODOGS PRESENT: STUFF WE ATE OFF THE FLOOR

RED APPLE 🐾

Only took one bite. Made us go blech. we give it one butt.

MYSTERIOUS PURPLE SUBSTANCE 🐾 🐾 🐾

we were too scared to eat it, so we made Toxic try it. Toxic made purple poops. we give it three butts.

ULTIMEATUM 🐾🐾🐾🐾🐾

Made of many meats. Made us gassy, but farts smelled like ultimeatum, so it was okay. we give it five butts for flavor.

FUN DIP 🐾🐾🐾

So. Much. SUGARRRRR! THREE BUTTS FOR MAKING US MOVE FAST.

KLEPTODOGS PRESENT: STUFF WE ATE OFF THE FLOOR

COTTON CANDY 🍑 🍑

Tasty, but the texture made us *feel yuck.* We give it two butts.

BEANS 🍑 🍑 🍑 🍑

Such protein. Much slime. The can got stuck afterward. Had to deduct one butt for poor packaging design. Still delicious. Four butts.

RUBBER CHICKEN 🐾🐾🐾

Not actually food, but we still bite it. Makes funny sound. Three butts for being almost food.

MAGIC TOADSTOOLS 🐾🐾🐾🐾

Mushrooms growing sideways. Pupper ate, now pupper walks on walls. Four butts for magical superpowers.

BAMBOOZLED PUPS

Whenever a pup gets tricked into wearing clothing, that pup has been bamboozled. Fortunately, these bamboozled pups also happen to look fine as heck. Take a peek at the most stylish pupperinos around in this section!

KLEPTODOGS' GUIDE TO FASHION

Food is always in style, so long as you don't eat it.

Imitation is the sincerest form of flattery.

For when you did a very BAD thing.

Being nerdy never looked so good.

KLEPTODOGS' DREAM JOBS

KARATE MASTER

Strong pup who has mastered the martial arts.
House Defense: 14/10
Intimidation: 12/10
Looks Cool: 16/10
Good Boi: 14/10

WIZARD

Powerful pup who can make food appear and squirrels disappear with a wave of its paw.
Magic Powers: 13/10
Charming Robes: 10/10
Confidence: 14/10
Good Boi: 12/10

FARMER

Country pup who can make you a salad on demand.
Farm Fresh: 12/10
Healthy Snacks: 11/10
Hardworking: 14/10
Good Boi: 12/10

BALLERINA

A posh pup who can dance circles around you.
Good Form: 10/10
Feel the Rhythm: 12/10
Classically Trained: 13/10
Good Boi: 11/10

KLEPTODOGS' DREAM JOBS

CONSTRUCTION WORKER

A strong pup who could build something for you, as long as you have the right permits.
Can Dig you a Basement: 13/10
Can Build Own Doghouse: 12/10
Passes Inspection: 14/10
Good Boi: 12/10

HEIRESS

A loaded pup who has the money to get what it wants.
Shopping Spree: 15/10
Pool Filled with Money: 13/10
Only the Finest Quality
Kibble: 9/10
Good Boi: 13/10

BUSINESS DOG

A Very Important Pup who is climbing the corporate ladder.
Stuck in Meetings All Day: 8/10
Has to Take This Call: 10/10
Cake in the Break Room: 16/10
Good Boi: 11/10

BIKER

A tough-looking pup who is sweet on the inside.
Rides a Hog: 16/10
Bad to the Bone: 12/10
Tough as Nails: 13/10
Good Boi: 14/10

STAGES OF SHOE POSSESSION

1. Pupper finds shoe.

2. Pupper chews shoe.

3. Human tries to take shoe from pupper.

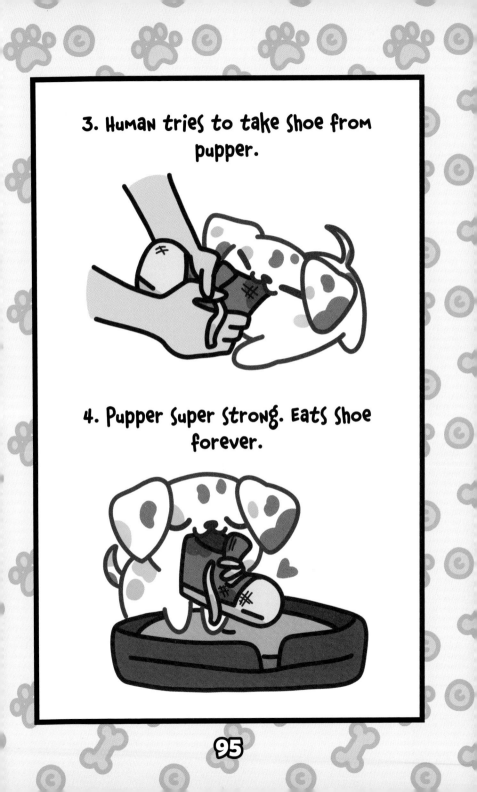

4. Pupper super strong. Eats shoe forever.

CONGRATULATIONS!

If you're reading this, that means you've made it to the end of this book. You're now fully armed to be the best fren a KleptoDog could ever ask for! You know the difference between floofers and yappers, corgos and woofers. You learned all about how to feed, groom, and care for your new pack, and you even learned what to do if your pups cause adorable trouble.

Give yourself a pat on the back—you deserve it!